THIS **Picture Knight** BOOK BELONGS TO

....

British Library Cataloguing in Publication Data

A catalogue record for this book is available
from the British Library

ISBN 0 340 53761 2

First published 1989 by Editions Fleurus, Paris, France, as *Kitou Scrogneugneu à l'école de Julien*
First published in Great Britain 1991 by Magi Publications, in association with Star Books International
Picture Knight edition first published 1992

Published by Hodder and Stoughton Children's Books,
a division of Hodder and Stoughton Ltd,
Mill Road, Dunton Green, Sevenoaks, Kent TN13 2YA

Printed in Hong Kong

**Picture
Knight**

HODDER AND STOUGHTON

SCRUFFY SCROGGLES

goes to School

by Ann Rocard   Illustrated by Marino Degano

Once upon a time, there was a horrible, hideous, slobbery little monster with six eyes, called Scruffy Scroggles. He lived in Station Road, Lilyville, in a suitcase under his friend Lucy's bed, and no one except Lucy knew he was there.

One night, when Lucy was asleep, Scruffy decided to go for a walk in the moonlight. So he climbed out of the window and walked for a long, long time, through the streets of Lilyville and then across the fields.

When the sun began to rise, the little monster decided it was time to go home, but he couldn't remember the way. Poor Scruffy was completely lost!

He hid behind a pile of logs and began to cry, great big green and yellow monster tears.

Then, suddenly, he heard a noise. A little boy was walking along with his satchel on his back, kicking an old tin can and muttering, "Won't go to school! Won't, won't, won't!"

Scruffy was fascinated. He followed the little boy at a distance, on tiptoe. Suddenly the boy turned round and snarled, "Why are you following me, you horrible hairy thing?"

"I'm not a horrible hairy thing," said Scruffy, "I'm a horrible, hideous, slobbery monster with six eyes and my name is Scruffy Scroggles."

"Mine is Stephen," said the little boy, as he took five marbles out of his pocket. "Would you like a game?" he asked.

"Okay," said Scruffy. "But why aren't you going to school?"

"I'm hopeless at lessons. Even my teacher says so," Stephen replied.

Scruffy nodded sympathetically, remembering his days at monster school. "I was always bottom of the class, too," he sighed. "I never made any spelling mistakes."

"I make lots!" cried Stephen.

"I never talked during lessons," said Scruffy.

"I do! I'm a real chatterbox," said Stephen.

"I never chewed my pencils," added the little monster.

"I chew the ends right off," replied Stephen. He couldn't get over it. What an odd school Scruffy must have gone to!

Then Scruffy told Stephen his story: how he had
left his terrible monster family to go and live with
Lucy, and how he had gone for a long walk in the
moonlight last night and ended up lost.

By now the little monster was very worried. He
wanted to go home to his friend Lucy.

Stephen scratched his head, thinking. "Lilyville?
Hm ... I'm hopeless at geography. Never even
heard of it! But our teacher might know where it
is. Follow me!"

Stephen took Scruffy's paw and led him along the road. Soon they came to Stephen's school, but there were no children in the playground. They had already gone inside – and the front door was locked.

Stephen pointed at the first floor. "That's my classroom, up there," he whispered.

"Let's get in through the window," suggested Scruffy.

Stephen and Scruffy helped each other up, and in no time they had climbed on to the window ledge and were signalling to the children in the classroom.

"Ooh, look! It's a caveman!" cried a little girl.

Mr Ali, the teacher, turned round. Eek! His hair stood on end. Eek! He waved his arms up and down. Eeek! He spluttered and he stammered. "Help! Help! It's an alien from outer space! Call the fire brigade, the ambulance, the police!"

At that moment, Stephen managed to open the window. He jumped down into the classroom smiling.

"Don't get all upset!" he said. "This isn't a caveman or an alien, it's my friend Scruffy. Can he stay for lessons? He won't make any noise, I promise!"

Mr Ali was so surprised, he didn't know what to do, so he decided he'd better carry on with the science lesson. Still trembling, he picked up his chalk and wrote the word *Cockatoo* on the blackboard.

The children were baffled. Cockatoo? What on earth did it mean?

Only one pupil in the whole class put his paw up. A horrible, hideous, slobbery pupil, with six eyes.

"I know what it means," said Scruffy. "It's a sort of parrot. My favourite is Leadbeater's Cockatoo, because it's so pretty. It's a white parrot with a red and yellow crest, which lives a long way away in Australia."

All the children clapped. "Well done!" they cried.

Even Mr Ali was impressed. What a clever monster! A big smile spread over his face.

"Now, can I ask you a question?" asked Scruffy.

"Go ahead," said Mr Ali.

"I want to go home to Lilyville. Do you know where it is?"

"Why, of course I do," said the teacher. "I can take you there this evening if you like."

So Scruffy stayed at Stephen's school all day. During games the little monster climbed to the top of the school porch and swung from rope to rope, letting out loud Tarzan yells.

At dinner time Scruffy went to the canteen with Stephen. His six eyes were gleaming greedily.

"I've got a monster of an appetite!" he said.

"Yuk! Fish and spinach," grumbled Stephen. "I hate fish and spinach."

"I love it," cried Scruffy, swallowing his whole plateful at one go.

"Yuk! Cheese and nut salad!" moaned Stephen.

"I love it," cried Scruffy, licking all the plates clean.

"Disgusting coconut cake!" complained Stephen.

"I love it," cried Scruffy, and he didn't leave a single crumb behind.

Stephen was amazed. Scruffy certainly did have a stupendous appetite!

After playtime, the children went back to their classroom. In this lesson, they had to write down poetry from memory.

"Oh, help!" groaned Stephen. "I can't remember mine at all."

What a good thing Scruffy was there! He knew the words of all the poems the children were supposed to have learnt, and he whispered the words they couldn't remember. The children were delighted – and just for once, Mr Ali pretended not to notice.

The school day was soon over. Out in the playground, all the children hugged Scruffy.

Mr Ali handed Scruffy a crash helmet and put
him on the carrier of his motor-bike. Brrrooom!
Off they went in the direction of Lilyville.
Stephen watched them go, waving and waving.

"Goodbye, Scruffy! Goodbye!" he shouted. "Come back and see me soon. You'll find me at school every day except Saturday and Sunday. I'm going to work really hard, especially at geography, so that I can find out where you live."

Soon Scruffy was back home in Station Road, Lilyville. He thanked Mr Ali and said goodbye. Then he climbed up the drainpipe and along the gutter, back into Lucy's room. Lucy was waiting for him. She had been so worried.

"Oh, Scruffy, I thought I'd never see you again!" she cried.

"So did I," said the little monster.

Scruffy didn't sleep in his suitcase that night. He snuggled under the eiderdown on Lucy's bed, and the two of them talked and talked all night long – but I mustn't tell you what they said.

That's their secret.